FIFTY SHADES OF GREEN

OR
COFFEEHOUSE CONFESSIONS
OF THE UNCOMMON JOE

JUDITH SESSLER

To my friend
and confidante
Judith Sessler
Hardy

FIFTY SHADES OF GREEN
OR
COFFEEHOUSE CONFESSIONS OF AN UNCOMMON JOE

copyright 2016 by Judith Sessler

ALSO BY JUDITH SESSLER

THE WORLD OF AIDAN McMANUS
copyright 2009 by Judith Sessler

BOTHERSOME BOBBY AND
THE TRAVEL KIDS
copyright 2016 by Judith Sessler

SAINTS AND SINNERS
short stories from the bizarre to the sublime
copyright 2016 by Judith Sessler

DEDICATION

For Charles and Kathy whose friendship I cherish

ACKNOWLEDGMENTS

There is a long list of people who need to be thanked for helping this book come to fruition and every one of them has the distinction of being a barista extraordinaire. Every morning while writing this book, I was welcomed with a hot mug of dark roast and a smile

First and foremost is Ramona who was the inspiration for the title <u>Fifty Shades of Green</u>

Next is Carol, who has been one of my biggest supporters

None less important are Danielle, Bob, Christina, Roni, Jordan, Dan, Jason, Justin, Arthur, Cody, Jess, Katy, Zach and Russell

TABLE OF CONTENTS

FRIDAY

CHAPTER ONE

Randy

Four-thirty in the morning was an ungodly time of day in mid-February. It was dark. It was cold. There wasn't a single, solitary person on the road apart from an occasional drunk or delivery man...and Randy. As assistant manager, she was on her way to open up the local coffeehouse. It was the place where the early risers, the ones who desperately needed a cup of coffee to jump-start their day, would congregate.

Randy's car was particularly persnickety that morning. After the initial click-click-click, the motor turned over and she cranked up the heater, even though she knew it would never actually heat up the car more than lukewarm. She really needed a new car and it was on her agenda: after she paid this semester's college tuition for her son, patched the roof on her 150 year-old house, paid off the new water heater...

Yes, she really needed a new car.

By the time she got to work, her fingers were chilled to the bone, even though she had on her warmest, wool gloves .

She turned the key in the frozen lock and eventually it opened. She turned on the lights using only the dimmer, in case there were any desperate customers hoping she'd open early.

She was always grateful when one of the other employees came in so she was not alone in the dimly-lit store. After all, there were a lot of whackos in the world nowadays.

4:45 am: time to get to work.

First things first. She donned the universal symbol of a designer coffeehouse, the green apron. She often wondered why *all* upscale coffeehouses wore the same bright green apron? They didn't even vary the *shade* of green. And when did a coffee *shop* turn into a "designer coffee*house*?" She knew it was when they started charging five dollars for a cup of joe and they started calling employees, 'baristas'.

After unpacking the boxes delivered the night before, and stocking the shelves and cooler, she checked the bathrooms to see if last night's crew mopped, cleaned, and replenished the supplies. There was nothing worse than a customer coming out to complain that there wasn't sufficient toilet paper.

...how embarrassing...

When you pay five dollars for coffee, you should be able to wipe your butt in comfort.

5:00 am: time to make the coffee. It's Friday, so the morning rush would be heavier than it was earlier in the week.

5:30 am: time to open the doors.

The first customer was always Jack. Every day he stood outside the door five minutes before they opened, no matter what the weather.

"Good morning, Jack," Randy greeted him as she poured his large black dark roast without needing to ask what he wanted.

Jack was *always* a large, black dark roast.

Next in was Tony. Extra-large with a double shot of espresso. He was a trucker on his way out for a 24 hour run so he needed the extra caffeine boost.

"Drive safe, Tony," Randy said.

The hallmark of a specialty coffeehouse - know the customers' names. The daily regulars automatically became part of the barista family.

Then there was the endless line of customers: latte after latte, cappuccino after cappuccino, espresso after espresso full-caf, half-caf, decaf, dry whip, no whip, 2 pump, 4 pump, light ice, extra ice...and so on and so forth.

9:30 am: Janice and her friends came in. Randy rang up the two medium caramel lattes, one 3 pump, one 5 pump, and one large, sugar-free, hazelnut cappuccino with non-fat milk. They took their coffees and sat down at a four-top near the front window.

CHAPTER TWO

Janice

Janice, Patti, and Barbara met every Friday morning without fail.

"Good God, it's cold out," Patti said.

"That's an understatement." Janice agreed.

"Could freeze the ears off a monkey," Barbara said.

They looked at her and cracked up.

"Where the hell did you ever hear *that*?" Patti asked.

"I dunno, but it's better than what I was *going* to say," she laughed.

They could easily imagine what *that* might have been. Barbara was the one who always came up with the most inappropriate things to say at a cocktail party. Particularly, when she'd had just a wee bit too much to drink.

"So, have you decided what you're going to do about Jerry?" Patti asked Janice.

"You mean my lying, cheating, son-of-a-bitch of a husband?"

"Yeah, that's the one."

"No, I haven't. Not yet. I've thought about calling his mother. That would fix his ass," she laughed.

Jerry was a momma's boy from the get-go. For infidelity, she would chew him up, spit him out, and then, use him for fertilizer. Not that she ever particularly liked Janice, but marriage was marriage and vows were vows. Besides, her own husband was a son-of-a-bitch too, so she wasn't about to tolerate the same outrageous behavior in her son. She was a strong-willed, controlling woman who didn't instill a sense of the warm and fuzzies, so she knew Jerry would react like a whipped dog with his tail between his legs. The image made Janice smile with perverse pleasure.

"Nah, that's stooping pretty low, to rat him out to his *mother*," Janice chuckled.

"I suppose you should probably take a more grownup approach. How about ripping the leather seats in his Lexus and stuffing them with oatmeal," Patti laughed.

"Good idea. If I did it when he was at the office, he'd have no clue it was me and he'd just be *really* pissed off."

"So he still doesn't know that you know?"

"No. He still thinks I'm his sweet, unsuspecting, gullible little wife. He's in for a big shock when I take out the artillery and start shooting."

"Just do me a favor," Barbara said. "If you're going to use real bullets, call me first. I wanna be there for the bloodshed."

Barbara's husband dumped her four years before for the cliché of a mistress, his secretary. She'd been tempted to take him out, but in the end, she settled for their mini-mansion, the Jag, the beach house, and a very nice monthly settlement that kept her well-stocked with Jimmy Choo's.

Janice knew she wasn't going to be quite so lucky. Her kids were grown and gone, she had a good paying job, and there were no extenuating circumstances other than the fact that her husband was a scum-sucking asshole.

Twenty-five years of marriage down the toilet, and she knew that was appropriate place for it to go.

They had just come back from a wonderful, romantic trip to St. Croix, where they walked in the moonlight, strolled on the beach with their toes in the warm water, danced to the tropical music in a local café, and made love that was reminiscent of the passion they felt on their honeymoon. It was a magical trip and Janice was still feeling the glow when they returned home.

The amorous attention Jerry lavished on her during their second honeymoon deceitfully lulled her into a false sense of security that her marriage was on solid ground. After 25 years, it didn't take much moonlit romance to renew Janice's belief that Jerry was still a faithful, loyal husband who was still in love with his wife.

Two days after their return, when Janice was still basking in the glow of their passionate second honeymoon, she inadvertently stumbled upon a crumpled receipt from an expensive restaurant she was unfamiliar with. She knew there was something suspicious because he never took anyone out to dinner except her.

At first, she was puzzled, then shocked, then devastated, then enraged, and eventually she was thinking of 50 different ways to castrate him. How could he have been so despicably deceitful on the beaches of St. Croix and then come back to someone else? ...someone who had to be young, sexy and beautiful, emphasis on the young... someone who worshipped him with puppy-dog eyes filled with the innocent, naïve, blind love of a twenty-something year old.

So she set her own natural-born devious mind into motion and did her own detective work. It didn't take much hunting. Jerry was pretty stupid, as far as an adulterer was concerned. It should have brought Janice some comfort that this was probably the first time, but it didn't.

She had been a trusting, faithful wife who devoted her life to her husband and family and now she was going to be discarded into a trash can like a pile of worthless garbage.

At her age, she wasn't sure she could be recycled.

Now she was just biding her time, making her plans, and waiting until the day she was going to pull the rug out from under him.

Maybe, she *would* tell his mother after all.

CHAPTER THREE

Jimmy

"Morning, Randy," Jimmy said as he pulled off his gloves.

"Good morning, Jimmy. How are you doing on this rotten day?" she asked her favorite customer.

It had started snowing and was coming down at a pretty good clip.

"Oh, c'mon Randy. I just love a blizzard. Don't you?" he laughed.

"Not hardly. With *my* car, it will be a crap shoot as to whether I make it home tonight or not," she chuckled.

Randy knew Jimmy, not just from the coffeehouse, but from the countless times he worked on her car over the years. He used spit

and glue and anything else that might work
in an attempt to keep it going just a little
longer. Jimmy knew she was in pretty dire financial
straits and he wished he could have helped her out
more.

She poured him a cup of Columbian in a
mug instead of the standard paper cup because
she knew he'd be there for a while.

He always came in on his days off. He sat in
one of the big, stuffed leather chairs with his coffee
and a book. He read for hours and refilled his coffee
cup several times. After his second mug, he
switched to decaf. He said too much caffeine would
make his heart do pirouettes, and unless they had a
defibrillator on hand, it would be better for all of
them if he skipped that third cup of caffeine.

"You doing okay, Jimmy?" Randy asked. He
seemed a little thinner these days and he was a
slight man to begin with.

"Yeah, just getting old," he chuckled.

He sat down, pulled the paperback out of
his jacket pocket and sat down to read.

Jimmy Musgrove was a tough guy in

his day. He was small but mighty. Despite his size, no one messed with him. It was hard to say if it was because of his hair-trigger temper or his small, but imposing presence when he got ticked off.

He had also been quite a ladies man. Decidedly handsome, with a shock of dark wavy hair and piercing blue eyes, he had no end of girls fawning all over him.

He loved the limelight. It stroked the ego that needed stroking because of his small-man's syndrome.

Jimmy didn't have the smarts it took to go to college, but was a wizard with his hands. He could fix just about anything and learned to become an ace mechanic at trade school. It served him well over the years and he had the reputation of being honest and trustworthy, two words that were rare in his line of work.

But he wasn't very successful in the relationship department. He married his first girlfriend, fresh out of high school. Bad move. He found out that neither of them were mature enough to live grown-up lives, even though they swore to their parents they were. Oh, the naïve delusions of a teenager.

They divorced after a year and were fortunate that their union produced no children.

His second wife came along 5 years later with a 2 year-old little boy in tow. Jimmy was more mature by then, but it didn't seem to make much of a difference. They divorced six months later. Luckily, the little boy didn't have time to get too attached.

His third and final wife turned out to be the love of his life. He was 32 and she was 30. She was a petite, dark-haired beauty with fetching green eyes. It was love-at-first sight for him and he finally found out what love was really all about.

They wanted to have a baby and finally, after three long years of trying, Angie conceived and gave birth to a beautiful baby girl. But as fate, mother nature, or satan, would have it, they both died in childbirth.

Jimmy was never the same. He closed up his heart and lived the life of a hermit, only leaving his house to go to work.

Years later, when he met Randy, he saw something in her manner that reminded him of Angie. It wasn't in her appearance. It was in her gentle spirit and it touched the tiny part in his heart that still had a spark of life in it.

So now, whenever he had a day off, he stopped in to read and have coffee. But truth be told, the real reason he went was to see Randy. In their five minute conversations, he would be reminded of the love that once graced his life.

As far as he was concerned, he would fix her car until the day he died.

16

CHAPTER FOUR

Mack

"Hey, Randy."

"Hey, Mack. The usual?"

His usual was a small frozen hot chocolate with a dollop of whipped cream.

"I'll drink whatever you want to give me Randy, and I won't complain if you give me something I don't like," he said as he made a goofy face at her.

Every Monday through Friday, Mack took the 9:45 am bus from home and arrived at 10:15 am on the dot. He sat at the counter, drinking his hot chocolate, and trying to talk to anyone who would listen to him.

But no one listened or talked to him. They felt sorry for him, pitied him and didn't want to hurt his feelings. They just wanted him to go away.

It hadn't always been that way for him. He grew up as the affable kid next door that everybody loved. He was the teachers' pet, the junior-high football team's mascot, and part of a group of teenage boys that called themselves 'the scoots'. They were avid skateboarders who hung out after school and on the weekends at the skateboard park.

So what changed to take him to the entirely opposite end of the social spectrum?

Through no fault of his own, or any one elses's, he was involved in a skateboard accident at the age of fifteen that left him moderately mentally handicapped.

Initially, Mack's friends felt sorry for him. He was one of their crowd. He was their friend. They spent hours together on their skateboards.

Now he was pitifully 'retarded' as far as they were concerned, and they were just a group of normal teenage boys ill-equipped to deal with the

19

situation.

It was very sad, but Mack was the guy that everyone avoided at all costs.

Randy was the exception. She was always kind and tolerant, no matter how irritating or annoying he was.

Her fellow baristas gave her props for being a saint.

Randy wasn't a saint. She was the sister of a severely handicapped younger brother.

Justin had a cord around the neck at birth and was born with severe cerebral palsy. He was wheelchair- bound and required complete physical care all his life. The saddest part was that he was mentally astute and had an IQ higher than hers.

Because of Justin's tragic circumstances, she had a natural affinity for the physically and mentally challenged. She knew that Mack was kind-hearted and gentle and had been robbed of the full life he should have had, just like her brother.

Mack liked to sit at the counter so he could talk... and talk... and talk to the busy baristas constructing a barrage of designer drinks for their customers. He never noticed they were too busy to converse while they were knee-deep in orders. Unlike Randy, they would, ever so pleasantly, grunt one word answers to Mack just to pacify him. His mentation was such that he was just as happy as if they engaged in a full-blown conversation. He really didn't know the difference.

It broke Randy's heart.

Mack's mother, Julie, was obviously devastated with the loss of the charming little boy that won everyone's heart. Now her life revolved around "raising" a son of 26 with special needs.

Julie and her husband Jeff were shattered by the accident. Mack spent many months in the hospital lying in a coma. When he came out of it, he spent the next two years in a rehab facility where they were able to teach him how to walk, how to talk, and how to dress and feed himself. He returned home able to physically function on his own.

Tragically, he was left with the mind of a ten-year old.

His father just couldn't cope and after a year and a half, he took off and Julie never heard from him again. Sadly, Mack never even noticed.

Julie was left to deal with the her son, the man/child, who could take care of his own daily physical needs, but couldn't be left alone, lest he burned the house down in an attempt to make popcorn.

His mother taught him how to take the bus every day to get his frozen hot chocolate. It was one of the few independent things he could do and he loved it because it made him feel like the grown-up he would never be.

Besides giving Mack a happy diversion, it gave Julie a much needed break. She loved her son desperately, but sometimes the strain was almost too much to bear.

She knew Randy watched out for him while

he was there and made sure to remind him when it was time to catch the 11am bus home.

God bless Randy. As far as Julie was concerned, she *was* saint.

CHAPTER FIVE

Alyssa

The snow had started to ease but it was still bitterly cold.

Randy was always baffled that anyone would want to brave the cold and snow just for a cup of coffee.

Personally, she would have preferred to stay nestled under a cozy, warm blanket in front of the wood stove at home.

But she knew that for some of the customers, the coffeehouse culture had little to do with coffee. Coffee was just a secondary benefit.

It was the atmosphere of urbanity and sophistication that the twenty and thirty-somethings craved. For the mere price of a cup of coffee, albeit an expensive one, they could feel like they were transported to a New York City café, hobnobbing with famous writers and theater people.

They would come and sit for hours, busily clicking away on their lap-tops and texting on their phones.

Alyssa was a creature of habit and had a favorite table. It was located away from the window so the noonday sun (if there ever *was* any) wouldn't reflect off the shiny, oak table and blind her. She arranged to take her lunch just before noon when there was a lull at the coffeehouse so her table would, most likely, be empty.

She came in, stamped the snow off her boots and put her briefcase down on 'her' table.

She ordered a chicken salad sandwich and her usual mug of decaf - with room. She already had two cups of caffeine at home and one at the office so she was already a little wired.

Alyssa knew she needed to come down a bit before she went back into the office. She had a three o'clock meeting and there was a lot riding on the presentation she was going to give.

Alyssa was a market research analyst for a computer software company. It was a plum of a job and she was ambitious to get ahead in her field.

She was efficient, self-motivated and creative. She had exactly the qualities that a VP of marketing needed. She worked long hours and put in her time to get noticed by her boss. He *did* take notice and recognized her superior business acumen.

She was on the fast-track towards management and had a bright future in the company...and it certainly didn't hurt that she was sleeping with the boss.

Their relationship was not purely one of sex. They worked closely together and over the span of two years he came to rely heavily on her. It was only natural they developed a relationship as friends.

Despite avidly maintaining their purely professional working relationship, they fell in love.

She didn't mean for it to happen. She wasn't some wide-eyed innocent who fell for an older man because he reminded her of her father, or because he was wealthy enough to become her sugar daddy. She simply let her heart rule her head and fell in love.

Unfortunately, Jerry was married... married for twenty-five years. They had just come back from an anniversary trip to St. Croix, a trip that Jerry said he felt very guilty about.

He told he was going to ask his wife for a divorce in the not too distant future, but in a perverse sense of loyalty, he felt he owed it to Janice to give her a memorable twenty-fifth anniversary. Something to remember fondly in the years to come.

Alyssa knew that Jerry didn't have a clue. You don't abandon your faithful wife of twenty-five years for another woman and expect her to remember *anything* fondly, especially the sham of a second honeymoon.

Alyssa had several disastrous relationships before Jerry. They all ended badly and left her with an aversion to fall in love again anytime soon.

Then Jerry came along, and that was that.

They often stayed late at the office under the guise of "working" and they knew no one suspected their clandestine affair. Only her best friend and confidante, Sara, knew about them.

They were, however, blissfully unaware that Jerry's wife found about them. Janice knew the *what* of it, but not the *who*.

Alyssa felt very guilty because it was never her intention to steal another woman's husband. She knew only too well the devastating havoc that it would cause because her own father did the same thing to her mother.

Her mother never recovered. She slipped into a deep depression and withered away from loneliness and grief. Then, after years of misery, she ended it all with a bottle of sleeping pills and a bottle of chardonnay.

Alyssa was so deeply engrossed in putting the final touches on her presentation that she barely looked up when the door opened and a cold gust of wind ushered in a dusting of snow.

She pulled her sweater around her shoulders and started putting her laptop in her brief-case.

As she put on her coat and headed towards the door, a woman passed her, saying, "forgot my credit card."

Alyssa froze, not from the cold, but from the fact that she was face-to-face with Jerry's wife, the face she recognized from the picture on his desk.

She nodded sheepishly at Janice and slipped out the door.

CHAPTER SIX

Roger

Randy had just finished her lunch, the one she brought from home because she couldn't afford the nine dollar ham and cheese sandwich that she could make at home for a dollar.

She put her apron back on and went behind the counter just as Roger came in. He looked frozen, in his letter carrier's uniform. She knew the trucks were barely heated in the winter and not air-conditioned at all in the summer. So he either froze or sweltered depending on the season.

"The largest, hottest cup of coffee you have for me, Randy," he said as his teeth chattered.

"You bet, Roger."

He took off his gloves to wrap his hands

around the cup in a futile attempt to momentarily warm them.

"Thanks," he said, and walked back out to his truck.

Randy knew it must be tough for someone his age to be out all day in such rotten weather.

It was a bitch of a day for *anyone* who had to work outside. The cold and snow were bad enough, but the wind blew through you like a hundred tiny little icicles.

Today, it was Roger's misfortune to have a walking route. On other days, on the *good* weather days, it was a blessing. He enjoyed walking the seven miles to deliver the mail. Except for the stray dogs that attempted to make a snack out of his ankles (and the rotten little buggers that actually drew blood), it was good exercise and it kept him in shape. He knew that he would be at least twenty pounds heavier if he ever switched to a driving route, but on days like today he was sorely tempted.

Roger worked for the post office for thirty-five years and was getting close to retirement. He wanted to hang on as long as possible to beef up his pension, but every winter was making it harder and harder. He had a couple of nasty spills in the past few years and was getting to the age when it wouldn't take much to break a hip. God, he hated getting old.

He started working at the post office right out of the army. It wasn't great money, but it was a steady job with decent benefits, and back in those days you could support a family on a modest income without the need for your wife to work.

His wife, Roberta, stayed home to raise their kids and was happy to do so. She was one of those women who actually *enjoyed* the idea of being a full-time housewife and mother. She was a June Cleaver type of mom who baked bread and cookies, darned socks (and who even knew what darning a sock *was* nowadays?), and hung sheets out on the clothesline so they would feel cool and crisp and smell of sunshine.

They had been married almost forty years and had a lifetime of both heartaches and joys, just like everyone else. Sometimes it felt as though the scales were a little unbalanced and tipped more in the direction of heartache, like when their son, Joey, was hit by a drunk driver and killed on impact. Their only solace was that he was killed instantly so he felt no pain.

But the scales tipped back again in the other direction with the blessings of their grandchildren. No one could ever replace Joey, but they often saw a reflection of his smile in his little son's face.

By the time he got home from work, his exhaustion was overwhelmingly evident. It was rough having to deliver mail in the dark with only a little flashlight in tow, but as the motto went... neither snow, nor rain, nor heat, nor gloom of night, stays these carriers from the swift completion of their appointed rounds... Roger would have liked to shoot the goddamn bastard who ever came up with *that* saying.

Roberta was a gem of a wife. On days like today when she knew how tough Roger was going to have it, she'd throw a hearty beef stew in the crockpot first thing in the morning. By the time he came home from work, the stew had caramelized and it's aroma infiltrated his senses the moment he opened the door.

Roger counted Roberta as the biggest blessing in his life and it wasn't only her cooking that elevated her to angelic status. She stood by him during the rough post-war years, during the financially lean years, during the heartbreaking, grief-stricken years and now through the growing into old-age years.

Whenever his melancholy mood struck, she would hit him with the 'you're only as young as you feel' line and she truly meant it. Despite the things in life that took a toll on her, she always had a bright, cheerful spirit and a naturally optimistic attitude. It was that sunny disposition that carried her through her own dark days to come out the other side unscathed. She was the yin to his yang, the Cheech to his Chong, and could easily lift his spirits when they needed it.

Tonight was one of those nights. She could tell he was weary of the day and at the moment he seemed weary of life itself.

He took a hot shower to warm himself up before dinner and it revived him somewhat.

He wasn't very talkative during dinner except to tell her how delicious it was and how much he loved her.

He kissed her goodnight and went to bed early because he was bone-tired and dreaded getting up for work the next morning.

When his alarm went off at 5:30, he didn't stir. She turned over to gently wake him, but still he didn't move. She went to stroke his face and give him a kiss, but still he didn't stir. And then she realized that he was gone. She knew the night before how he was weary of life and almost seemed ready to give up the fight.

Tears rolled down her cheek as she laid her head on his chest, but she knew he was finally at peace and reunited with his beloved Joey.

CHAPTER SEVEN

Randy

It was finally time to clock out and Randy reminded herself that the extra money she made working overtime was well-worth the exhaustion, the ache in her back, and the swelling of her feet that made them feel like sausages in her shoes.

She passed the barista torch on to Noah, a bright young (emphasis on the *young*) man who was working very hard to get his speech pathology degree. The evening baristas were mostly young college students who had no problem going to school all day, working at night, and then for some of them, partying after work. Randy envied their stamina and determination, both of which she no longer possessed.

She closed her eyes, held her breath, and

said a little prayer to the car-starter gods that her tired old Camaro's engine would turn over. She always chuckled when the 'youngsters' she worked with commented how *awesome* she was to own a Camaro, even though it was eighteen years old. They didn't know that she would have gladly traded it in for a reliable little Civic. They didn't know that the relic she drove was a remnant from years past when her bum of a husband ran off with a teenage chickie of dubious character.

She married Kevin when she was twenty-one and he was twenty-five. She was enamored by the manly qualities he possessed: a tall build with broad shoulders, muscular arms, and a flashing white smile. She didn't heed her mother's warnings that he changed jobs with clockwork-like frequency and never picked her up on time for their dates. He was often hours late, without so much as a phone call or explanation.

Still, smitten as she was, she married him anyway. She never wanted to admit to her mother just how right she was, but when the electricity and heat were turned off in their tiny, one room apartment on a regular basis, she had to swallow her pride and go to her mother for help. There was many a time when the only thing in her fridge was a case of beer for Kevin, and *she* existed on peanut butter and ramen noodles.

The only consolation she had was that he never hit her. When he got drunk, which was pretty much a nightly occurrence, he would storm out of the apartment and end up in some dive bar in a disreputable part of town.

When she got pregnant with Noah, she knew she finally had to admit that her 'marriage' was a disaster of monumental proportion and went back home with her tail between her legs.

Her mother never said "I told you so" and she welcomed her home with open arms.

Eva's heart broke for her daughter. She wanted only the best for her, but she was very wise and knew Randy had to live her own life, learn her own lessons, and live with the consequences of the poor choices she made.

By the time Noah was born, Kevin ran off with 17 year-old Addie, who was pregnant with what she *said* was his child. Maybe yes, maybe no.

At first Randy was devastated, but in the end, she knew Kevin was a bum and she and Noah were far better off without him.

Her mother considered it a blessing when Randy moved back home. Eva had plenty on her plate taking care of Randy's brother who needed continuous care, 24/7. She had a system and an established routine in place. A home health aide came each morning to bath, dress, feed and get him into his wheelchair. Eva took care of him for the rest of the day until evening when an aide came to to put him to bed. Randy stepped in to help ease the burden on her mother as much as she could.

Justin was nineteen when his sister moved in and he was ecstatic to have her back. Growing up, she was his champion. She navigated getting him through elementary and middle-school and then the more difficult task of high school.

He was smarter than most of the kids at school, but they thought he was 'retarded' because of the uncontrollable sounds and body movements he made when he attempted to speak. Only someone who spent a lot of time with him could understand what he was saying and most of the time that person was Randy. He was teased and ridiculed by kids who were callous and cruel to a boy who was both physically and emotionally defenseless.

If it hadn't been for Randy's staunch defense, Justin's spirit would have simply withered away. Instead, he thrived, and thanks to the adaptive resources of computers, he was in his third year of college when he developed an antibiotic-resistant infection and slipped quietly away, the night before his twenty-second birthday.

If it hadn't been for Noah, Randy and Eva's grief would have been unbearable, but he made them laugh and raised their spirits as only a three-year old little charmer could.

Now, years later, Noah was away at college and her mother retired to Florida. At night, after work, she sat alone wondering where all the time had gone? Shouldn't there be more to the rest of her life? She thought maybe she should take a night course somewhere...in something...in anything...expand her horizons... plan for a different future, but the reality was that she would never have enough mental or physical energy after work to go back to school. And far more importantly, she would never have the money.

She made herself a cup of chamomile tea before bed and was ever so grateful she had the next day off.

SATURDAY

42

CHAPTER EIGHT

Zach

Zach dragged himself out of bed, took a quick three minute shower, pulled on the jeans he wore the night before, put on a clean flannel shirt and headed out for work. His roommate, Ryan, was still passed out on the couch from a hard night of partying.

Zach regretted, from day one, letting Ryan move in. They had been acquaintances in high school and he seemed like a decent guy back then, so Zach figured he would make a reliable roommate.

Unfortunately, he made the wrong call. Granted, Ryan *did* pay his share of the rent and other expenses, but that was as far as his reliable qualities went.

It turned out that Ryan was a hard-drinking, pot-smoking, sex-seeking party animal, the exact opposite of Zach.

Zach Randall was what any parent would label the *perfect* son. He listened to his parents, followed the rules, never skipped school, always did his homework, and never stayed out past curfew. He graduated with honors from high school and never gave his parents a moments worry that they might receive a late-night phone call from the authorities.

Yes, he was perfect in every way...except that to his parents disbelief, he was gay.

Greg and Carol Randall were the quintessential, middle-class, suburban parents. They belonged to the PTA, volunteered at school fund-raisers, enrolled their son in football, baseball, Boy Scouts, and attended every event Zach participated in. They went to church every Sunday and sent him to their church-sponsored summer camp every year.

As far as Greg and Carol were concerned,

they did *everything* right. So they could not understand, nor could they accept their son's decision to become gay.

Zach tried to explain that he didn't *decide* to become gay. It was who he was and always had been. From the time he was a young adolescent, he knew. He also knew that it would be totally unacceptable to his parents. They would never accept him for who and what he was, so he didn't tell them. They never seemed to notice that he didn't date or have a girlfriend. They were actually grateful that he devoted himself to his studies and extracurricular activities.

It was purely by accident they found out that Zack was gay. At a summer church picnic, their pastor, inadvertently, within earshot of his parents, asked Zach if he had found a boyfriend yet.

Months before, Zach sought out Pastor John's counsel to reconcile his homosexuality with the rest of his life and he found the pastor to be surprisingly helpful and understanding.

So he couldn't comprehend what could *ever* have possessed him to bring it up at a church function. His parents were so distraught and mortified that they left their church in embarrassment and shame, and they disowned their only son.

From that time on, Zach had no contact with his parents...or the church.

Zach loved the early morning shift on Saturdays. The place was so busy he didn't have a chance to ruminate on anything unpleasant in his life. He could forget about his parents. He could forget about Ryan. He could forget about the fact that there was no love interest in his life because he wasn't looking for one-night stands or hook-ups.

He didn't frequent gay bars or parties. He wasn't flagrant about his sexual orientation. He was simply living a normal, conventional life, looking for a serious committed relationship. His parents, and a good portion of 'straight' society, would never understand that just because he was gay, he still wanted the same things a heterosexual person wanted...a monogamous, permanent relationship. The only difference was that *he* needed it with another, equally committed, man.

"Hey, Zach, how's the situation with Ryan going? You throw him out yet?" Gabe asked, as he pulled a double ristretto espresso for the next customer in line.

"No, he's never sober enough for me to have that conversation with him," he chuckled.

"Maybe you should leave him a note attached to his packed suitcases," he said, half-seriously.

Gabe and Zach were hired within a week of each other and became close friends. Zach shared his confidences with Gabe without judgement. Gabe played it a little closer to the chest and wasn't quite as forthcoming with all the aspects of his life.

Zach knew he had it pretty tough.

Gabe's mother was a hard-core junkie who lived on the streets, prostituting herself just for a dime bag. Gabe tried to play the dutiful son and rescue her from herself, but he knew it was no use. She had OD'd more than once and he knew it was only a matter of time before she was found dead in some alley with a needle in her arm.

"Well, if you ever get him out of your place, let me know. I'm ready to get the hell out of where I am. I'm *done*. I can't do it anymore," Gabe said, sadly.

That was all Zach needed to hear. He would do *anything* to help Gabe get out of his situation. He was going to go home and kick Ryan's ass out of his apartment.

Zach hoped that moving in with him would give Gabe a chance at a better life. He deserved it.

They *both* did.

"Two small hot chocolates, two medium coffees, and two chocolate chip cookies, please."

"Sure, sir" Zach smiled at the man.

He didn't feel it was polite to call an elderly gentleman by his first name. That was the just the way he was raised.

It would have made his parents proud.

CHAPTER NINE

Adam

Adam took the tray of hot beverages and bag of cookies to the table where his wife and two granddaughters were sitting.

"Grandpa, did you get us cookies??" Lily asked excitedly.

"Cookies? You didn't want cookies, did you?"

Lily's face fell.

"Don't tease her, Adam. Of *course* he did," his wife, Vickie said.

Lily and Grace both smiled ear to ear as Adam handed them each a cookie and their hot chocolates.

"Thank you Grandpa," they said in unison.

"Thank Grandma, too."

"Oh, thank you, Grandma." they said with their mouths stuffed full of cookies.

Vickie laughed as she watched them gobble them down with lightening speed. She remembered their mother doing the same thing when she was their age. This morning she was remembering old, sweet memories and making precious, new ones.

"Grandma, when are Mommy and Daddy coming home?" Grace asked.

"They'll be home tomorrow. They'll be there when you get home from school."

"Yay!" Lily smiled.

Lily and Grace were six-year old twins and had never been away from their parents for more than a few days. It was a special treat to be with Grandma and Grandpa for a whole week, because as their mother told them, they would be spoiled rotten...she was right.

They couldn't wait to tell their Mom and Dad; Grandma baked oatmeal cookies and let us help; we made pink and orange tissue paper flowers for you; they took us to the movies, *twice*.

As much as Grace and Lily missed their parents, they would be sad when their grandparents left. They knew it would be a long time until they saw them again because they lived so far away. They wished they still lived around the corner.

They moved to Florida when Adam retired from his job of forty years as bank manager.

He started as a part-time teller right after he graduated from college. He knew he had to start at the bottom and work his way up the ladder, but he hoped it didn't have to be on the very bottom rung. Well, so be it. At least it was a steady job with good benefits and a future. He knew he would be able to advance with some rapidity because, number one, he graduated with a 4.0 and top of his class with a BS in business, and number two, his father was president of the bank.

Adam felt only *slightly* guilty it was nepotism that propelled him upwards in his career, but he got over it quickly. He knew he was the most qualified and the best man for the job...and his father knew it, too.

Being the pragmatic sort of guy he was, Adam made sure his financial future was secure before he asked Vickie to marry him. They had been dating for over five years and she was getting impatient, but she knew he was a practical man with a goal and a plan. And nothing *ever* deterred him from his plan, especially anything or any*one*, motivated by emotion.

So, Vickie waited...and waited...and waited, watching all her friends marry and start families, trying hard not to become resentful. She knew Adam wouldn't be rushed into anything before he knew their marriage was going be unwaveringly stable. As much as she loved him, she wished he had more of the spontaneity of her friends' husbands. What she really wished for, was for Adam to whisk her away to Vegas and elope on a whim. But Adam had never done *anything* in his life on a whim. And he never would.

His one year plan was to marry and buy a house in the suburbs.

One year plan accomplished.

Five year plan: two kids, promotion to head teller.

<u>Five year plan accomplished.</u>

Ten year plan: promotion to bank manager, upsize their home to a more affluent community.

<u>Ten year plan accomplished</u>.

Fifteen year plan: secure childrens' college educations, secure future retirement.

<u>Fifteen year accomplished</u>.

And so on and so forth until the forty year plan was accomplished and they retired to Florida.

Vickie didn't really have anything to complain about. Adam was *exactly* the same man he was when they married. There were no surprises along the way. Everything was carefully planned out and there were never any ups and downs. He was a good man. He just didn't have a romantic bone in his body.

Vickie would have loved an emotional component to her marriage, but it was what it was...a steady, stable partnership, solid as a rock... and just as dead.

So, craving an emotional connection and knowing that it just wasn't something Adam was capable of, she did what any self-respecting, loyal wife of forty years would do... she had an affair.

Vicki met Chip at the same coffeehouse where they took the grandkids for their hot chocolate and cookies.

Vickie's morning treat, and guilty pleasure, was to sit and drink a cappuccino every morning after Adam left for work. It was the one indulgence she allowed herself. Adam had a structured budget and she was given a weekly allowance that he believed was adequate for her needs. At first she felt some guilt spending five dollars every morning for a cup of coffee. Five days a week, five dollars a day...twenty-five dollars a week...a hundred dollars a month...twelve *hundred* dollars a year.

Adam would have been *appalled,* so she never told him. It was her secret, and once she reconciled herself to the fact that she squirreled the money away out of her own allowance, she felt guilt no more.

She sat in one of the two soft brocaded chairs near the window. In the beginning she would just gaze out and daydream. She imagined what a different sort of life she would have had if she married differently. After all their years of marriage and at the ripe old age of sixty-four regrets served no purpose.

Then one day, Chip sat in the chair next to her, first asking if the chair was occupied.

He startled her out of her daydream. She looked up and shook her head no, it wasn't.

Chip was a tall, thin man with a shock of gray, wavy hair and watery blue eyes. He was wearing jeans and a blue Yankees sweatshirt. She judged him to be in his late sixties, early seventies. He had a soft voice and pleasant face.

"Thank you," he said as he sat down and opened his newspaper.

She just nodded and smiled.

That's how it began...quietly...guilelessly... unintentionally.

Every morning at nine o'clock, she came in and sat in her usual chair and he came in fifteen minutes later. She put her purse in his chair so no one would sit in it.

It started innocently enough. She looked out the window and he read his paper. After several mornings of sitting silently, he struck up a conversation about the weather. Then, once the floodgates were opened, they talked about everything, from their backgrounds and their families, to the bygone hopes and dreams of their pasts.

They developed an emotional bond that went far deeper than anything Vickie ever had with Adam. They began to share their most intimate feelings and one thing led to another.

After six months of their emotional affair, it blossomed into the physical.

At first Vickie thought, I'm a sixty-four year old married grandmother with saggy breasts and saddlebags. What on earth could he see in me?

Chip thought, here I am, an old man of seventy-one, with spindly legs and hanging skin. What on earth could she see in me?

It wasn't so much what they *saw* in each

other. It was what they felt. Chip lost his wife of forty-eight years to cancer several years before and was terribly lonely. Vickie was in desperate need for her empty love tank to be filled, even if it was only a little bit.

They continued their relationship for the two years before Vickie and Adam moved to Florida. They were both deeply saddened to leave each other, but they knew right from the beginning that it had to end eventually.

While it lasted, Chip gave Vickie the love she desperately craved all years with Adam, and it was enough to last the rest of her life. Now her daydreams were filled with fulfillment and not longing.

When she heard Chip passed away quietly in his sleep a year after she left, she silently mourned the man who was truly her soul-mate and the love of her life.

"Grandma, what are we going to do today?" Lily asked, breaking Vickie out of her reverie.

"Anything you want sweetheart. Anything

at all."

"We can do whatever your heart desires," she said and hugged her tightly.

CHAPTER TEN

Morgan, Taylor, Pepper and Zoë

"They're here," Zach muttered to himself when the 'snot squad' walked through the door.

No one knew his nickname for them, but if they did, they would have agreed.

The four teenage girls were quite the group. They all came from affluent families who instilled in their daughters that they were special and deserved all the privileges that their parents' upper-class status afforded them. They were openly rude, showed no respect for anyone below their class level, and knew for certain that their shit didn't stink.

They were groomed from an early age to believe they *deserved* the best in life. Theirs was a life of entitlement. They were being groomed as the next generation of the privileged elite by virtue of their birthright alone.

"Large iced caramel chip with extra whip," Morgan said, as she handed Zach a fifty.

He marked it with the pen designed to determine if it was counterfeit.

"You've *got* to be shitting me. Counterfeit? *Really*??" she said as she rolled her eyes and looked at her friends.

They all rolled their eyes in unison and laughed at Zach.

He smiled and handed her the change and thought, remember Zach, you get paid to put up with this crap.

Next up - Zoë.

"Same," she said, smirking as she purposely handed him another fifty.

Same routine. Same response. Same eye rolling.

Next up - Taylor.

"Same," and handed him her fifty.

Zach was a very tolerant person, but these girls could test the patience of Job...maybe even of Jesus, as well.

Last up - Pepper.

She was the only one of the four who had a modicum of decency and the only one who didn't hand him a fifty.

"I'll have a medium, iced green tea, please," she smiled, almost apologetically for her friends.

Zach didn't know *why* she was different, but he appreciated it. He wondered why she hung out with the others. He suspected it was peer pressure or parental expectation to hang out with the 'winners'.

Whatever the reason, he hoped she would be able to break free of their sickening influence before it was too late, but she seemed to be under their spell.

They took their drinks and sat down.

As they sipped their drinks, they put their heads together and with furtive glances and obnoxious whispers, they laughed at anyone they felt was comical in their eyes.

All except Pepper. She kept her head down, slowly sipping her tea, so she didn't have to partake in her friends' ridicule of others.

Pepper came from a different background than her 'friends'. Even though her father was an important corporate CEO making tons of money, he always remembered his humble roots. Ethan's father was a blue-collar worker who scrimped and saved every dime he could to send his son to college. In the end, Ethan earned a full scholarship to Harvard and his father was able to put the money he saved towards his own retirement.

Ethan worked hard for what he had and took nothing for granted. He tried to instilled those values in his daughter, but knew he was fighting an uphill battle. Because he was part of the CEO echelon, he was automatically accepted in the elevated social circles and that meant Pepper was too.

He knew she was having a hard time. She wanted to fit in, yet she had such conflicting beliefs.

He didn't know that she cried into her pillow at night because she felt trapped in a dichotomy of values with no way out. Either she went along and belonged, or she broke free and became a target of their cruelty.

It was a lose-lose situation and the pressure was becoming too hard to live with.

"C'mon, let's get out of this dump," Taylor said, and left her cup that was dripping residual whip cream on the table. It was beneath her to dispose of her cup in the trashcan that she passed on the way out.

Morgan and Zoë did the same and followed her out. Pepper lagged slightly behind, picked up their cups and threw them in the trash.

Zach watched her and smiled when he caught her eye.

She was a nice girl and really hoped she would be able to *survive,* but he had his doubts.

SUNDAY

CHAPTER ELEVEN

Audrey

The sun was finally starting to shine after three miserable days of wind, cold and snow. Audrey loved how the reflection of the sun glistened on the snow as it peaked it's head above the horizon.

On a morning like this, she was glad she didn't have to be in to work until later in the morning. She was always up long before her husband, so she could enjoy the peaceful, almost spiritual moments sitting in front of the wood-burning stove in her pajamas.

She sat, hot mug of coffee warming her hands, thinking about her boys. They were both grown and gone and living far away from home.

Thomas was an electrical engineer who lived in North Carolina. Liam lived in California and was still trying to find himself.

She missed them both and wished she saw them more often, but they had their own lives to live. As much as she would have liked to have more influence in some of the questionable choices they made, she knew they had to find out the consequences for themselves.

Thomas had just relocated to North Carolina with his girlfriend of three years. He secured a high-paying job with a good future, depending upon the economy of course. His girlfriend, Nikki, transferred to a nursing program at Duke and was due to graduate at the end of the year.

Audrey was glad he was finally settling down with Nikki after having been in several disastrous relationships. Thomas was her stable one.

Liam, on the other hand, was the child she worried about from the time he was two. He was the rambunctious one who pushed the limits of everything, from jumping off the top bunkbed and breaking his wrist, to doing wheelies off a rock wall on his bike and needing 15 stitches under his left eye. To this day, he still proudly wore the scar as a badge of bravery.

His current escapade was joining a rock band in Frisco despite the fact he had no musical talent, *whatsoever*. God bless him. He lived in an old, six bedroom house that he shared with the members of the band and several other people of questionable character.

Audrey was glad he only shared the basics of his life with her, and *not* the details.

God, please protect him. He needs it.

Despite the sunshine, it was colder than Audrey expected, so she went back into the house to grab her heavy knit scarf. Gary, her husband, had just woken up and was pouring himself a cup of coffee.

"Hey, hon. Wasn't sure you were going to get up at all," she laughed.

"Yeah, I'm still trying to recoup from

Friday's all-nighter."

Gary did landscaping during the good weather and snow removal in the winter. As much as he hated the physical strain and the ensuing exhaustion, the money was good and helped them make it through the winter.

She kissed him on the forehead and left for work.

Sunday was an extremely busy day at work. There was such a wide cross-section of people coming and going. They came in droves before church and then again after when it let out. There were couples dressed up and on their way to whatever Sunday function they had. There were the young, avid sports enthusiasts going out to tackle mother nature...skiers, snowboarders, skaters...

Audrey had long since given up thinking there was anything pleasurable in outdoor sports and had no desire to rekindle the spark. Leave it to the young and hearty.

"Refill dark roast, please, Audrey."

"Sure, Nate. How are you doing?" she asked as she handed him back his mug.

"Not too bad. You know my saying...any day above ground is a good day," he laughed.

He truly meant it.

CHAPTER TWELVE

Nate

Nate took his coffee and went to sit back down with his friends, Joe and Sam.

They were his friends from childhood and had always been thick as thieves. All through school they stuck together, no matter what. If one of them got in trouble, they all took the blame. When they graduated, they all applied to the same paper mill and declined the jobs when only two of them were hired. They found a machine shop that hired all three of them and as long as one of them stayed, they all stayed.

Audrey thought of them as the coffeehouse's own Three Musketeers.

Every Sunday, without fail, they met for coffee and fellowship. Every Sunday except for the ones they spent helping Nate through his cancer ordeal. They still met, but it wasn't for coffee.

Nate felt a lump in his neck and thought nothing of it. It wasn't sore and it was small enough that he forgot about it. He didn't even mention it to Marion, his wife. It wasn't until she noticed his face seemed a little thinner that she asked him if he felt all right. He said he was feeling a little tired, but he was putting in extra hours at work to save for their summer vacation.

A week later, Marion became concerned. It was obvious he lost a little more weight. He had a thin face to begin, but he was beginning to look gaunt.

He told her about the tiny lump which now felt a little larger to him. She had him at the doctor's the next day.

From there things went quickly.

Biopsy

PET scan

Bone marrow aspiration

Hematologist

Medical oncologist

Radiation oncologist

Radiation

Chemotherapy

Nate was the kind of guy who never complained. Even when he broke three fingers on his left hand at work, he just taped them up and finished his shift.

He was healthy as a horse, his wife used to say, which was in stark contrast to her many minor, yet legitimate, illnesses.

So she was desperately distraught when he was brought down by the cancer. She felt helpless to do anything but console him and even then she had a hard time concealing her fear.

It was Sam and Joe, the two other Musketeers who came to Nate's rescue.

They alternated taking time off from work

to bring him to his radiation and chemotherapy treatments.

They sat with him during his four hour long chemotherapy infusions and brought his heavy fleece blanket to keep him warm.

They held the puke buckets when necessary.

At first the nurses were confused. Marion went to his initial chemo treatment, but needed smelling salts to revive her. She had no illusion that as much as she loved her husband, she was ill-equipped to deal with anything related to his life-saving treatments. *She* knew it and so did he.

He completely understood because she had been that way since childhood. She even passed out when they had their pre-marital blood tests. His only concern was how he would manage it all without her.

His fears were quickly laid to rest when his buddies stepped in. Whether it was his weakened condition, his gratitude, or both, he was brought to tears.

It was a long, painful, arduous ordeal, but

they persevered and Nate was in remission.

Now here it was two years later. They returned to their Sunday coffee klatches, laughing, chewing the fat, talking about everything from who was going to the Super Bowl to the state of world affairs.

Audrey knew the story and had great respect and admiration for the friendship they shared.

And she knew that when they ordered, Nate always picked up the tab.

78

CHAPTER THIRTEEN

Reuben

Audrey was glad to see Reuben come in. He was her favorite co-worker. He was a pleasant hard-working *barista*. The job title always made him laugh.

"Hell, I make *coffee for gods-sake.* I'm not a swarthy Italian in tight jeans making espresso in an outdoor café," he chuckled.

Reuben always made her laugh.

"Hey, pretty lady," he winked at her.

His greeting could never possibly be construed as having a sexual connotation.

It was just his way of making her smile.

...Reuben was as harmless as a fly...

He had a very disarming smile and she thought he'd make a nice match for Carly, the other barista working that night.

He certainly *was* no swarthy Italian. He was shorter than Audrey by an inch with red curly hair and a sweet angelic face that any mother could love.

"Hey Benny. It's been crazy today. I haven't had a chance to refill the soap containers in the bathrooms."

"Well, you shouldn't be in the men's room anyway," he chuckled.

"I try my hardest *not* to," she laughed.

"Drive careful. It's a little slippery out."

"I will," she said as she took off her green apron and put it in the laundry bin.

Reuben watched her leave and told Carly he was going in to stock the bathrooms.

It was early evening so there was a different type of clientele. It was mostly students working on their computers or after-work socializers. The mood was always quieter as the evening wound down.

It was an unusually slow evening, so he and Carly had a chance to talk about things they couldn't have if more customers were present.

"What a jerk that guy was last night. Wait until I see Liz! If that's her idea of a nice guy, then she needs to learn to raise her standards," she laughed.

"Not a gentleman, huh?"

"Creep is what he was."

"Sorry you didn't have a good time and that he wasn't the man of your dreams."

"More like he was the guy my nightmares are made of."

Reuben couldn't have been happier. He had been in love with Carly from a month after she started working with him. But he had no illusions that she could ever be interested in a short, redhead with a smattering of freckles who reminded most people of a garden gnome.

From the time he was little, women would pinch his cheeks and squeal, 'isn't he *adorable? Just look at those dimples!'*

He was always teachers' pet which served him well in elementary school because he could get away with all sorts of mischief. Even if he was sent to the principal's office, she would be persuaded to lessen her reprimands when he flashed his impish grin at her. Sadly, it never worked on girls.

Reuben never had a girlfriend, and he had long-since resolved himself that he wasn't on any girl's short-list and probably never would be.

He simply wasn't a guy that girls found attractive. He was easy to talk to, listened to their confidences and wouldn't laugh. Girls treated him like a brother, and they knew,

...Reuben was as harmless as a fly...

It was fifteen minutes before close. They started the routine of putting food in the walk-in and milk in the fridge near the espresso machine. They hoped they had seen the last of any stragglers wandering in for a cup of coffee.

"Crap," Carly said as the glass door opened

and a guy in a heavy green parka with a sheepskin-lined hood walked in.

He walked up to the counter and Carly's attitude changed. When he slipped back his hood, she was looking at one of the hottest guys she'd ever seen. His bright green eyes bore right through her. He was tall and she could tell he sported a muscular physique even through his bulky jacket.

"I hope it's not too late," he said in a velvety voice.

"No, no problem at all," she said, even though it meant a delay in breaking down the equipment.

"Would it be too much trouble to make me a latte? Whatever is easiest for you," he said politely.

"Not at all," she smiled as she looked into his hypnotic green eyes.

She would gladly give him whatever he wanted.

Reuben watched from the background with a frown. He saw Carly melting to this stranger's magnetism.

He was used to girls falling for the hunks,

the sexy guys, the six-foot muscle-bound athletes, falling for anyone but *him*.

"Thanks," he said, in a voice dripping with sexual innuendo.

"Have a good night," she said, hoping he'd come back sometime.

He put his hood back up and left.

Carly was still smiling to herself as she started breaking down the coffee machines.

Reuben watched the guy walk to his car thinking, why couldn't I be that guy?

His sleek black car was parked next to Carly's in the darkened part of the lot. He got in and sat in the driver's seat without turning the car on. Reuben saw the glowing end of a cigarette. All the while, the car remained off.

Reuben kept watch as he swept the floor. He had a creeping sensation that there was something ominous about the guy. Quietly, so as not to alarm Carly, he went to the silent alarm and pressed the button.

The man was still sitting in the darkened car when three cop cars sped into the lot, lights flashing and sirens blaring.

There was a loud crash when Carly dropped a tray of mugs on the floor.

"What the hell??"

They watched as two officers pulled the man out of the car and handcuffed him.

"Oh, my GOD!" she whispered.

The first car sped off with the man safely handcuffed and contained in the caged back seat.

The other two officers came to the door. Reuben unlocked it and let them in.

"Which one of you hit the alarm?" the first one asked.

"I did," Reuben said.

"Good call. We've had this guy on our radar for months. He's wanted in three states for suspicion of kidnapping, rape and murder."

Carly's knees started to buckle and Reuben caught her just before she hit the floor.

One of the officers pulled out a vial of smelling salts from his pocket and waved it under her nose.

She was cold, clammy, and white as a ghost.

Knowing she was in shock, the other officer called for an ambulance.

She was still unable to speak.

"You need to thank this young man for his radar and quick thinking. He probably saved your life," the one with the smelling salts said to her.

Carly looked up at Reuben.

It turned out Reuben wasn't harmless as a fly, after all.

MONDAY

CHAPTER FOURTEEN

Randy

As assistant manager, Randy automatically received a call from the police the night before. She was shocked speechless.

Poor Carly!

Thank God for Reuben!!

After the call, she was unable to sleep. Every time she closed her eyes, she envisioned Carly being dragged off and thrown in the trunk of a car. She imagined the horrible things that would have happened to her if it wasn't for Reuben's intervention.

She was late getting to work, but excused herself due to the circumstances. Jack waited patiently for her to open the door. He heard about

Carly's close call on the early morning news.

"Is she okay?" he asked.

He knew Carly from the mornings she worked the opening shift.

"I don't know for sure. I'm going to give her a little time to sleep before I call her. Actually, I think I'll call Reuben first."

"They must be pretty shaken up."

"I can't even imagine," Randy said, honestly.

Nothing so alarming had ever happened in their small town before. It was the kind of thing you heard about in the cities. The entire town would be on edge. Their safe haven was abruptly and disturbingly rocked to the core.

Well, tell Carly I'm thinking about her when you talk to her," Jack said.

"Will do, Jack. See you tomorrow."

The coffeehouse was abuzz with the happenings of the night before. It was the front page headline in the local newspaper and the first story on the morning news.

Reuben was, rightly so, touted as a hero. She would make sure that his name went up on the board as 'barista of the month'. She decided she would erase 'barista' and replace it with 'hero'.

Randy knew that Reuben, of *all* people, who was shy and unassuming, would be terribly embarrassed with all the attention.

She was right.

Reuben followed the ambulance to the hospital and sat at Carly's bedside until the shock wore off and he was able to drive her home.

"Reuben, I don't know how I can ever thank you. You saved my life. That guy seemed okay to me," she said, embarrassed that she was terribly attracted to him and would've accepted a date if asked. She shuttered when she thought about it.

He walked her up into her apartment and made her a can of chicken soup. It was what his mother always did when he needed comforting. It was all he knew to do. What he *really* wanted was to put his arms around her and stroke her soft brown hair.

He sat with her until she fell asleep, kissed her on the forehead and left for home.

Carly was startled awake when she heard the door close. She sat bolt upright and ran to the window. Reuben was just unlocking his car door.

In a panic, she opened the window and yelled to him.

"*Reuben! Rueben!!*"

He looked up and saw her leaning out of the window.

"Please don't go! *Please,* don't go!" she cried.

Reuben ran back up the stairs and found her sobbing in her open doorway.

"It's okay, Carly. You're safe."

He put his arms around her and walked her back to the couch. She laid down in his arms, crying softly. She fell asleep with Reuben holding her. He stayed awake the entire night, holding her, stroking her hair, and protecting her from harm.

Randy called Reuben on his cell phone, unaware he was still with Carly. He said she was doing much better and he was going to stay for as long as she needed him. He didn't tell Randy, but he was hoping that would be for a long time.

Randy told him she had both their shifts covered that night and if they needed more time off to let her know.

The rest of the day was busy with customers that talked about nothing else but the 'police action' from the night before. Women were shaken and men flexed their masculine egos and talked about what *they* would have done to the bastard.

Right before the lunch rush, the local news station sent a reported and cameraman to interview the staff and customers.

…what did they think about this situation? Did they feel safe in their community now? How do they think Carly felt? Did they think Reuben was a hero?…

All pretty stupid questions. How the heck

did they *think* anyone felt?

By the time she was ready to leave, the fervor died down and things were pretty much back to normal. She double-checked that the night staff knew how to trip the alarm and told them the police were going to be around at closing time to walk staff to their cars.

When she felt assured that everything was under control, she left.

She walked out to her car and double-checked four times that there was no one lurking around. She never had to do that before. She knew the face of their lives would never be quite the same.

TUESDAY

CHAPTER FIFTEEN

JACK

For the first time in forever, Jack was not waiting for Randy when she opened. She had a flicker of concern and then realized her motherly instincts were kicking in. Even though those instincts shouldn't apply to her clientele, she knew they did anyway. She was just that kind of person. She was a gullible, soft-hearted woman who was a sucker for a sob-story or any person with their hand out, even when it meant foregoing something she needed or wanted for herself.

She watched the door every time it opened, expecting it to be Jack, but Jack wasn't going to be coming in that Tuesday.

"Jack, where the hell *are* you?"

"Be right there, Mom. Just getting your tea."

"Well, hurry it up!" she barked.

Jack poured the water in her favorite mug- the one that said '*worlds best Mom*'. He rolled his eyes and brought her the tea.

Jack Gilpin was what most people called a momma's boy. He lived with her his entire life. He shopped for, cooked for her, did her laundry, took her to the doctors and anywhere else she wanted to go. Jack did *whatever* she asked. He never had a girlfriend, or any friend, for that matter.

Yes, he was a momma's boy, but not by choice. He hated his mother with a passion that could set the world on fire. He couldn't wait for her to cross over to the other side, and he knew she would need sunscreen for where she was going.

Alice Gilpin was an evil woman...not just your ordinary run-of the-mill nasty woman...she was *truly* evil. When Jack was five and didn't finish his dinner, she locked him in the pantry until breakfast. He never left anything on his plate again. When he forgot to feed his puppy on time one morning, she packed Max up and took him to the pound to be put to sleep. She made sure Jack knew what she did and that it was *his* fault. He cried into his pillow for weeks, muffling his sobs. If his mother heard him, she would have beaten him with a wooden spoon in places that didn't show the bruises. She was careful to make sure his bruises *never* showed so they would go undetected at school. She was an expert at it.

"Get me my toast. And don't burn it!" she yelled, when he brought her the tea.

Yes, Mom," he said with the patience of Job.

Once he became an adult, he learned to completely tune her out in order to protect himself from either going crazy, or killing her, whichever came first.

The only escape he had was his job at the

gas and electric company. He worked Monday through Friday in the billing department. He *was* the billing department, so he basically worked alone and that's just how he liked it.

The only thing he looked forward to was seeing Randy every morning. It was only a few moments of polite banter, but it was the only real connection he had with humanity, and he cherished it.

Jack had been so traumatized in his childhood that he withdrew into his own private world, devoid of outside relationships. He learned to find comfort and escape in books. He could transform his mind to inhabit other worlds: worlds of fantasy: worlds of whimsy: worlds of the past: worlds of the future: worlds that were outside the realm of his very present, very horrific reality.

Jack was extremely disturbed that he couldn't go to the coffeehouse that morning. It unbalanced him. He wasn't grounded when his morning routine was disrupted.

His mother woke at four in the morning

screaming for him. She had a leg cramp and needed his help. She *always* needed his help for something. She had him run a bath and make her a cup of tea. By the time he finished settling her back into bed, it was too late to go for coffee. She slept until half an hour before he needed to leave for work.

He made her tea and toast and then sat down at the desk in his bedroom to make some decisions about his future.

He was forty-eight years old with nothing to show for life and nothing to look forward to. His books offered him the only respite from his pain, but it was becoming increasingly difficult to find any solace or peace.

Jack called in sick, something he never did because his job gave him the only opportunity to escape his mother's venom.

"Why are you still here?" his mother growled at him.

"It's okay Mom. I have some sick time on the books and I wanted to spend the day with you."

"What the hell for?" she snarled.

What the hell for, indeed.

Jack made himself useful doing several loads of laundry and then went to the store to pick up some groceries. He wanted to make something special for lunch.

He set the table and brought in the lunch tray. He made his mother's favorites, tomato soup with ham and cheese sandwiches, and tapioca pudding for dessert.

She sat down at the table and for a brief moment there was a softness in her eyes that quickly turned to cruelty. She was a bitter, evil old woman without a heart.

"Drink your tea Mom," he said sweetly and without an ounce of regret.

It was several days before they found the bodies. The poison was in the tea. There was no note and there was no one to ask... why?

Randy didn't know it, but sadly, she was the closest thing to a friend Jack had.

And even *she* wouldn't ever know why.

CHAPTER SIXTEEN

Janice

It was unusual to see Janice on a Monday and without her usual side-kicks, Patti and Barbara.

She took her latte and sat at a small corner table in the back, far away from the other occupied ones.

Randy thought she seemed a little distracted.

It was just before eleven and she greeted Alyssa when she came in. She glanced over and saw that Alyssa's table was unoccupied so she knew she would be happy. It amazed Randy that people were such creatures of habit and something as simple as a table change could throw them for a loop.

Alyssa sat down with her coffee and sandwich and took out her laptop to do some work.

She was mid-bite in her sandwich when Janice pulled up a chair and sat down.

Alyssa's face turned beet red and she couldn't swallow.

"Hello, Alyssa," Janice said, syrupy-sweet.

"He...hello," Alyssa managed to whisper.

"So, I understand that you're the whore who thinks she's going to take my husband away from me," Janice said in voice dripping with honey.

Alyssa wanted to slide under the table. The people sitting around them at the nearby tables were busy drinking coffee and chatting away, so she didn't think anyone heard Janice.

"Well?" Janice repeated.

Alyssa was beside herself. She felt the acid in her stomach rise up in her throat and remained speechless.

"I'll bet you have plenty to say to my husband...words of love...words of devotion. And I bet he has plenty to say to you, too. I bet he's told you that you're the love of his life, his soul-mate, the woman he's waited for his entire life. I bet he's promised to be faithful and loyal, and to cherish you forever."

"I bet he's told you that his wife doesn't understand him and that she never has. I bet he's told you he only stayed for the sake of the children. I bet he's told you he can't live without you."

This time, several people turned their heads, hoping to hear the one-sided conversation.

Alyssa didn't know what to do. Her things were spread out all over the table so she couldn't just get up *run*...run from the embarrassment...run from the humiliation...run from the truth.

Jerry *had* said all those things to her. Whenever she was in his arms, she *knew* how much he loved her. She *knew* he would be faithful and loyal because she was the love of his life. She was his soul-mate...because that's what he *told* her.

He said he was going to ask Janice for a divorce as soon as he felt the time was right. It wasn't right, *quite* yet. Their son was flying home for her birthday in a few weeks and he would ask her right after he went back home.

He had been telling her for the past year that the time wasn't quite right.

Alyssa felt a cold shiver go down her spine that had nothing to do with the glass door that just opened.

Her mind was racing. She was thinking of things she never considered before. Could Jerry just be stringing her along? Had he been lying to *himself* when told her she was the love of his life?

More importantly, had he been lying to *her?*

Was it *all* a lie? Was she the quintessential cliché of a mistress who believed her lover's empty promises?

Suddenly, the pieces of her life started shifting. She was becoming painfully aware that what she believed was reality, was nothing more than a sham. Jerry was *not* going to leave his wife. All this time, he had been stringing her along.

She was shaken back to the situation at hand when she realized the monumental mistake she made.

"I'm so sorry," she whispered to Janice and hung her head in both anger and shame.

"Sorry for what?" Janice asked, already knowing the answer.

"For believing him. For being part of his betrayal to you. I feel so ashamed. I'm going to break it off as soon as I see him," Alyssa said, believing their marriage would be saved.

"Don't bother, Alyssa," she chuckled. "*I* certainly don't want him anymore. I just filed for divorce and you're *more* than welcome to him," she laughed, as she stood up.

"Be grateful that *you* won't be sitting here twenty years from now telling some young, gullible girl the same thing."

Janice felt the brisk, cold air hit her in the face as she left. Out of the corner of her eye, she saw Jerry's car pull into the lot.

Must be meeting her for lunch, she thought.

By the time she got to her car, she was laughing so hard she almost wet her pants.

CHAPTER SEVENTEEN

Jimmy

"Hi, Jimmy," Randy said when he came in.

"How ya doin'?" he asked.

"Not bad," she answered, as she handed him his coffee.

"I heard about the other night. Pretty scary."

"You said it. Everyone's really still shaken up. Reuben's coming back to work tonight, but I told Carly to take the rest of the week off, with pay."

"Good decision and very nice of you."

"It's the least we could do."

"Not all bosses would be so understanding. Most of them only care about the bottom line."

"Well, I had to clear it with the higher-ups, but I think they figured it makes for good public relations."

"Yeah, bad press is a bad thing," he chuckled.

"That's for sure," she laughed.

It was one of the things he most admired about Randy, her ability to do the right thing. She had that rare special gift to empathize and act accordingly. It was a quality he didn't see in many people. She had no idea how much he cared about her friendship.

As a mechanic, the people he saw were pretty oblivious to him, as if he were an inanimate object like the wrenches in his toolbox.

He was just a necessary means to an end... fix my car and do it as cheaply as possible...and make sure it never breaks down again...

"You haven't called lately, so I'm assuming your car's been okay."

"Yeah, it's made it a whole week without trouble," she laughed.

He took his coffee and went to sit down with his book. He was only able to stay an hour because he had a doctors appointment.

Ever since Angie and their baby died, he avoided doctors and hospitals like the plague.

It was time for his yearly checkup and he would have blown it off, but he was tired and really starting to feel his age. He thought maybe some vitamins would perk him up.

It's tough to get old, he thought, but it sure beat the alternative.

CHAPTER EIGHTEEN

Randy

It was the end of a *very* long week for Randy.

The entire Reuben/Carly ordeal left her spent. Besides dealing with the media frenzy, she had to reassure and comfort the staff, then tell and re-tell the story to the continuous stream of astonished customers and then she worked double shifts to cover for Reuben.

She was exhausted and wanted nothing more than to go home, turn off her phone, and take a nice hot bath.

As luck would have it, her car had other plans for her.

"Goddammit it! You have *got* to be kidding me!" she yelled out loud. She looked around to make sure there was no one else around to hear her take the Lord's name in vain.

She sat in the driver's seat with her head resting on the steering wheel. She was too exhausted to move or to think.

She sat there for five minutes before she tried turning the engine over again.

Nothing.

She wanted to cry, but she was even too tired for that.

She finally had to concede that her car was just as tired as she was. Probably even more so.

It was getting colder inside the car and she was shivering by the time she pulled out her cellphone to call Jimmy.

"Jimmy I am *so* sorry," she started to say, but he interrupted her.

"Are you at work or home?"

"Work," she said, flatly.

"Be right there."

She put her head back down on the steering wheel and sobbed.

What would she ever have done without Jimmy? He didn't hesitate for an instant. When she needed him, he came. No matter what time of day or night, no matter what the weather, no matter what he was doing, he came to her rescue. She only wished she could do something for him in return, to repay the kindness that went far above ordinary friendship.

Randy saw his truck pull into the lot not more than ten minutes later.

She breathed a sigh of relief and thanked God for him.

"Jimmy I'm so sorry to drag you out..."

He put up his hand to signal her to stop.

"There was nothing on tv anyway. I hate those goddamn reality shows. If I see one more red rose I going throw the damn thing out the window," he laughed.

She laughed at the thought of him watching *The Bachelor.*

He was tinkering with his tools and fiddling with some wires.

"I don't think this old relic has much more life in it, Randy."

"I know, I know. Will you look around for an old clunker that might last me long enough to…"

To what? she thought to herself.

She had no resources, no savings, nothing to fall back on. It was hopeless. She knew she would have to find a way to get to and from work and the thought was daunting. The early morning buses just didn't run early enough.

While she was ruminating on the thought that she might have to take up residence on a cot in the back room at work, the engine turned over.

"Thank god. I didn't think I was gonna get it started," Jimmy said.

"No, thank *you,* Jimmy, and as for me, you're as close to God as I'm going to get."

She kissed him on the cheek and he watched her drive away.

EPILOGUE

Randy

When she got out of the taxi, she wished the weather was better.

The storm clouds loomed overhead and the cold wind was blowing the dead leaves around. The frozen ground was hard and cold against her feet. She was wearing boots, but the cold went right through them.

It was a long walk. She wrapped her scarf tighter around her neck, but it didn't help much to keep out the chill.

As she approached the cemetery plot, her eyes welled-up with tears. She was sadder than she had been in a very long time. This was a tough blow. This loss was almost too much to bear.

How was she going cope?

The wind was blowing in her face, freezing the tears on her cheeks.

The sun was making a desperate attempt to peek through the fluffy, gray clouds. She looked up, as if to will the sun to shine through and shed some light on the gloom she felt in her aching heart.

There was only a handful of people at the graveside and the only flowers were the ones she sent.

"Oh, Jimmy. Jimmy," she whispered softly as she wiped away the tears.

Her heart was breaking. She stood silently thinking to herself. I'm going to miss you Jimmy. You were more than a friend to me. You never knew just *how* much you meant to me and now you'll *never* know.

She walked to the plain wooden coffin and placed a red rose on the top. She thought he would be amused since the last thing they talked about was the red rose.

She turned away, sniffling back the tears, when a man in a dark grey overcoat approached her.

"You're Randy, aren't you?" he asked.

"Yes."

"This is for you," he said, and pulled out a white sealed envelope with her name on it.

"What is it?" she asked.

"I don't know, but I was instructed to give it to you," was all he said, as he walked away.

Randy sat on her bed with the envelope in her hand, still reeling with the emotion of the day.

Slowly, she ripped it open and took out the contents. There were two papers.

The first was a letter from Jimmy.

Dear Randy,

*If you are reading this, then I have gone to
a better place. Please don't be sad. I had as good
a life as one could expect. Life threw me some curves
and some heartaches. But, all in all, I was content at
the end.*

*And that was because of you, Randy. I never
told you how much you meant to me. You were always
a kind and gentle person who made me feel like I
wasn't alone in the world anymore.*

*My life was lonely after I lost Angie and the
baby, but you brought me back out of myself enough
so I could find some peace at last.*

*Please don't ever forget how much you
changed my life, and remember me whenever you
think that you don't matter.*

God bless you, Randy
Your friend,
Jimmy

She couldn't control her sobbing. It seemed to go on forever. When she was finally able to calm herself down, she went to the bathroom and splashed cold water on her face. She looked in the mirror and saw the reflection of a grief-stricken woman who just lost the best friend she never knew she had.

She went back to read the other letter in the envelope.

LAST WILL AND TESTAMENT OF
JAMES L. MUSGROVE

Randy stared down at the paper in disbelief. Jimmy had left her everything. He had an insurance policy of $100,000, a policy he had taken out after he met Randy. He left her his three bedroom house and his share in the repair shop he co-owned.

But the most important thing he left her was something she would cherish forever.

a brand new car.

ABOUT THE AUTHOR

Judith Sessler's love of writing began as a child. She wrote poetry on napkins and short stories in her school notebook. Her first published works were essays and magazine articles when she was in her early twenties.

She took a writing hiatus of five years when her family moved across country and she pursued a career as a restaurant manager.

When they moved back East, she discovered that her husband, inadvertently, had discarded the box which contained everything she had ever written.

Judith was so devastated, she was unable to write another thing for over twenty-five years.

Then, unexpectedly, she woke up in the middle of the night with a book title in her head. That was how it always happened, a title in her head at night and the stories flowed from there. The rest is history.

Judith's books run the gamut from romantic fiction, to juvenile fiction, to short-story collections, to this latest endeavor which was inspired by the "office" she writes in every day...Starbucks

60619133R00080

Made in the USA
Middletown, DE
02 January 2018